Moshi Monsters™

Pick Your Path

Disco Mystery

1

SUNBIRD

Published by Ladybird Books Ltd 2011
A Penguin Company
Penguin Books Ltd, 80 Strand, London, WC2R 0RL, UK
Penguin Group (USA) Inc., 375 Hudson Street, New York 10014, USA
Penguin Books Australia Ltd, Camberwell Road, Camberwell, Victoria 3124,
Australia (A division of Pearson Australia Group Pty Ltd)
Penguin Group (NZ), 67 Apollo Drive, Rosedale, Auckland 0632,
New Zealand (a division of Pearson New Zealand Ltd)
Canada, India, South Africa

Sunbird is a trade mark of Ladybird Books Ltd

By Lauren Holowaty

www.ladybird.com

ISBN: 978-1-40939-077-0
2
Printed in Great Britain

To claim your exclusive virtual gift,
go to the sign-in page of

MOSHIMONSTERS.COM

And enter the eighth word on the ninth line
of the seventeenth page of this book!
Your surprise free gift will appear
in your treasure chest!

It's the opening night of the Fizzbangs' sensational *You Rox!* tour, and you're at the Underground Disco watching a really sticky warm-up jamming session. You can't wait to see the Fizzbangs rock the house, or to take to the stage yourself for the Moshi Annual Scare-Guitar auditions! (Scare Guitar is just like air guitar, only scarier.)

"You rock!" you yell at the top of your lungs, jumping on another monster's shoulders, peering over hundreds of adoring fans in the mosh pit. You catch a glimpse of the big-headed Katsuma, Axl Van Slap. The Fizzbangs' ever-so-famous and fiery bass player is at the side of the stage practising his 'I'm-too-cool-for-you-all' smile.

Axl spins around and gives you a 'I know I do' roxstar nod. He's always ready to rock his incredible monstar attitude and you love him for it! If it was up to Axl though, he'd probably ditch the rest of the Fizzbangs and be a one monster band.

Behind Axl, the rest of the Fizzbang gang are backstage getting ready to pluck, bash, tinkle, scratch and yell their way to gig glory right in front of you. You're so excited!

The usual backstage shenanigans are going on. An

entire scare-dressing team are backcombing the Furi drummer, Thwack's, hair. Missi Tinkles is twiddling her twinkly fingers, so she can strike the right chord with the audience. DJ Demonsta is mixing up all the tunes (hopefully he'll get them in the right order before they get on stage). Riff Sawfinger, ace Zommer guitarist, is winking his one eye at the roadies, and lead singer Avril . . .

But as you look closer, you spot that something's not quite right. You can't see Avril Le Scream, and everyone looks a little panicky, including the security guards, who are there to keep everyone calm. Could the Fizzbangs possibly have stage fright after all these years of performing? Something strange seems to be afoot.

"Screeech, BANG!"

Suddenly, the warm-up band's music stops and the stage is cleared. The lights go out, and Tyra lets out a very loud "Ahhhhhh!" (Being a screamtastic Fizzbangs fan, she just couldn't help it.)

Plunged into total darkness and eerie silence, the monstrous crowd of fans around you, start whispering about what must be going on.

"Shwoo, woo, woo, woo!"

"Shweee, shwurp, sweening, schwee."

"Psp, psss, psp, psp!"

Somehow, you gather from the Mosh pit whisperings that this isn't a dramatic start to the hottest band in the land's concert, but that you were right – Avril Le Scream is missing! Last seen at her make-up mirror, lip-glossing to the max, she never made it to the side of the stage to warm up her vocal chords.

'Maybe she just needed more Glueberry lipgloss?' you think. 'She probably just popped above ground to get some. No need to worry.'

The emergency lighting sparks on and Roary Scrawl jumps on stage to do a live satellite slink-up for *The Daily Growl*. "Listen up Moshis. This is a headliner headline! See what I did there, clever, huh?!"

The audience groans and starts chanting, "Get on with it!"

"Anyway," continues Roary, realizing rock fans are a tough crowd to please, "Avril Le Scream has disappeared. Mr Crumble, the Fizzbangs' band manager has cancelled the concert. Without Avril, there will be no more noise . . . sorry, I mean no more rock music, tonight folks."

Once again the audience groans, "Nooooo!" and starts chanting, "Fizzbangs! Fizzbangs! Fizzbangs!"

Roary listens to his earpiece and carries on, "I am now hearing reports that there will in fact be no more music played in Monstro City AT ALL, until the leading Poppet has been found. I'm afraid that this means the Scare Guitar auditions have been postponed as well."

Shouts of "What a Monstrocity!" and "Scare Guitar Rox!" are heard from the crowd.

You look over at the Scare Guitar judging panel, by now Tyra Fangs is crying her heart out, (Roary is on stage of course) and Simon Growl does not look happy. He hasn't come out of his mansion tonight to judge nothing. He surges towards the front, leaps onto the stage, and howls,

"Monster madness! The audition must go ahead no matter what! Music in Monstro City may be banned, but all the world's a stage and the show must go on! We shall simply move the Scare Guitar event to Rockstar Reef. Now who's got Scare Guitarist talent?!"

"Me, me, me!" cheers the crowd, literally raising the roof in 'I wanna be a star' excitement. "We love you, Simon!" Followed by, "Even if you are quite mean!"

"All those still wishing to enter the audition," continues Monstro City's greatest (and only!) talent scout, "must set sail on the *CloudyCloth Clipper* and head to the reef, immediately!"

Monster mayhem and crazy crowd chaos ensues, as the entire audience of wannabe Scare Guitar superstars race for the exits to the Underground Disco, and stampede their way to The Port in search of monstardom.

"It seems everyone was here merely for the auditions, not for watching the Fizzbangs," you say to ... well yourself, really, as everyone else is too busy leaving.

When everything calms down, you look around and realize that it is just you and Dustin Beaver left in the Mosh Pit, staring at an almost empty stage. Dustbin is singing along to himself, without a care in the world.

'Could have been worse,' you think. 'At least Beaver has cool dance moves, or is that Dustbin Whataflake?' You're into ear-splitting rock, not floppy-haired pop, so they all look and sound the same to you.

"Hey!" you hear from the stage. "Are you gonna help us find Avril?"

It's DJ Demonsta standing on stage with Thwack, Riff and Missi Tinkles. (Axl had obviously decided this was the perfect opportunity to start his solo career, so had made his exit earlier on.)

"I'm in!" cheers Dustbin, starting to break into song again, "I never say never!"

"What about you?" says Thwack, pointing his great big roxstar paw right at you.

You really want to be a Scare Guitarist, but you also want the opportunity to hang out with a totally cool rock band. It's a pretty monstrous decision to make. What will it be?

If you decide to run to The Port, **turn to page 51.** After all, you haven't been practising Scare Guitar every day for years and years, to miss out on an opportunity of a lifetime!

If you decide to stay put, **turn to page 60.** You have been following the delightful diva that is Avril and her rocking band for years now and you'd hate to see the band never play again.

The Fizzbangs all decide to become celebrity Super Moshis for the day, mainly because they like the outfits, and they head off with the Super Moshi top team to champion peace, justice and find Avril, of course!

"Dustbin will keep you company," shouts Thwack on his way out, almost as loudly as he thwacks his big bass drum.

"Thank you!" you cry and you find yourself a place on the floor to watch the Super Moshis live on the big screen.

A fellow monster hands you some Slopcorn, and you begin your Super Moshi couch mash potato adventure.

It's just like being at the Monstrodeon Cinema! You see the Super Moshis race back towards the Underground Disco to investigate. The Fizzbangs follow closely on the Super Moshis' tails, literally on their tails, so there is some tripping and falling involved, but still everyone looks so cool, wearing their bright red masks and capes.

"Go, Super Moshis!" you cheer at the screen.

Next, the Super Moshis find a note inside the drawer of Avril's Vanity Table. Some words pop up on screen, 'Vanity Table available from a Yukea store near you.' You can't quite see what the note from the table says, but you see the team zoooooom off into a maze of underground tunnels, full of music.

The team race through the intertwining spaghetti-like tunnels, meet lots of people, search for clues painted on the walls, barrel roll under gates, take a crazy cart ride that brings them back above ground and eventually end up face-to-face with Dr. Strangeglove.

"What is Dr. Strangeglove doing there?" You wonder.

Just as things get really exciting, and you see the Super Moshis trying to distract Strangeglove, you also get your first glimpse of Avril who he's holding hostage. Then something flashes onto the screen, so you can no longer see the action . . .

" . . . Marketplace – Spring, Summer, Autumn, Winter Sale – NOW ON!'

"Not an advert, now!" you gasp.

" . . . Packed full of boutique shops to suit every monsters' needs," continues the voice on the ad.

Then, the advert snaps to another,

"Don't miss Goof Morning Moshis TV on at 7am every day this week, next week and probably every week forever more. This week's special guests include the glamorous Cherry Goal, and then all eyes (even his own) will be on Roary Scrawl. It's the perfect scary start to any monster's day. Goof Morning Moshis and welcome to a brand new day!"

"C'mon! I want to see what the Super Moshis are up to!" you growl at the screen, but all you are shown are adverts.

After a long time, the screen finally goes back to the Super Moshis.

"Mission complete!" you hear Missi Tinkles cheer on screen, accompanied by a few keynotes on her piano.

"What?" you gasp, "What happened? What did I miss?"

Turn to page 77.

"We'd be at capacity! All ye remaining Scare Guitarists, stay put, yarrr!" shouts Captain Buck E. Barnacle.

But you squeeze yourself on-board the *CloudyCloth* anyway, just as it is about to leave.

As the ship sets sail, you look back at the monsters on dry land, waving their arms, desperate for a shot at the auditions.

"Phew!" you gasp, "Made it!" You can't help feeling a little pleased with yourself. After all, you are now sailing off towards your destiny as a Scare Guitarist superstar.

Trying to find some space to practise your moves, you realize that the boat is Fango Mandango jam-packed. There's not even room to swing a Catacactus!

You perch carefully on the edge of the poop deck.

"BANG! BANG! SPLASH!"

"What was that?" you ask.

"Monster overboard!" you hear Cap'n Buck's shipmate, Lefty, cry out from the crow's nest.

"Monster overboard!" Lefty shouts out again and again, pointing in all directions.

"Woooaaa!" You start sliding to one side and realize that the *CloudyCloth* is capsizing!

The ship is evacuated and everyone piles into lifeboats.

"Looks like there'll be no auditions this year," howls Simon.

You and your fellow Scare Guitarists may be safe, but your dreams have come to a watery end. Well, at least until next year! At least you have your souvenir Scare Bear!

THE END

You, the remaining members of the Fizzbangs (Axl is long gone) and Dustbin Beaver, head out of the Underground Disco in search of the Underground Music Tunnels.

'Avril did say that she wanted to take her music underground, so she has to be here somewhere,' you think.

It's very dark, so you're glad Thwack finds a Tentacle Torch tucked behind his Furi ears, along with his drumsticks! He uses it to help light the way.

The tunnel walls are slimy and covered in bat droppings from Wing, Fang, Screech and Sonar, the Underground Tunnel's premier bat residents.

Just as you're about to say something about the stench, Wing flies into your face.

"You looking for Avril?" he screeches, so high pitched you can barely understand him.

"Yes, why?" you ask.

"I'm sure we've seen her crying in the tunnels down here!" screeches Sonar.

"Crying?" you ask, worried that Avril may be scared or upset.

"Well, I actually think it's her singing," screeches Fang, "Sonar just hears things so loudly, she gets confused sometimes."

"We think she was heading to the Underground Music Tunnels," screeches Screech.

"Yes, but where are the tunnels?" you ask the batty bats, but not one of them answers.

Just then, you turn a corner and hear music pumping all around you, very loudly.

You ask the bats which way Avril went at this point.

"Left or right," reply Wing and Fang together

"Right or left," reply Screech and Sonar together.

"Thanks for your help," you reply, not really meaning it.

It's a simple dilemma, but which way do you turn? Left or right?

If you turn left, **turn to page 43.**

If you turn right, **turn to page 75.**

But then it dawns on you . . .

The Scare Guitar Competition never actually happened, as Simon Grow and the *CloudyCloth* never left The Port. Which means you didn't need to go to Rockstar Reef, and you could still be a superstar Scare Guitarist one day. Phew! Everything is monsterliciously fine!

Plus, you have a sneaky suspicion you know where Avril Le Scream is. You remember that the Gift Island Ferry normally drives itself, and how many sailors do you know who use the phrase 'monstar-licious', like fine dining, night-time water skiing, stargazing and hanging out at Rockstar Reef?

Once everyone dries off on land – since they only have wet toes from the small amount of water, it doesn't take too long – you announce that you might just know where Avril Le Scream may be.

You look over at the ferry captain and give her a knowing wink. She pulls off her captain's outfit and reveals her fluffy white fur and starry eye.

"AVRILLLLL LE SCREAM!" everyone screams, almost as loud as the lead-singing Poppet herself on the Fizzbangs' 'He Screams, She Screams, I SCREAM LOUDER' new single.

"Hooray!" "You found her!"

You are given a knight-hoodie for your heroics saving the passengers of the *CloudyCloth*, and the whole of Monstro

City are delighted that you found their beloved Avril and convinced her to go back to her first love – standing on a stage, with a band, pretending to sing, but really just screaming as loudly as she can.

The peppy-razzi hound you every day, trying desperately to get a picture of your monster mug – as you're totally an M-list celeb now if ever there was one.

'And to think, all I wanted to be was a Scare Guitarist,' you think to yourself, staring at your famous face in the mirror each morning.

THE END

You open the door, and as soon as you step into the Chamber of Screams you are bombarded with thousands of, **"ARRRRGGGGHHHHs!"** and **"FREEEEKs!"** and **"YEAH, YEAH, YEEEAAHHHs!"**

Then it's your turn to scream, **"YOUUUCH!** My poor ears!"

You, the Fizzbangs and Dustbin search the chamber looking for Avril. You put your paws over your ears to shield them from all the screaming, DJ Demonsta puts his headphones on, Thwack sticks his drumsticks in his ears, Missi Tinkles distracts herself playing her keyboard, and Riff puts his crazy long tongue in one ear and smoothes his long purple locks over the other.

The only one who doesn't appear to be at all bothered by the screaming is Dustbin,

"I'm so used to all my fans screaming at me in the street," Dustbin explains, "this is just like a normal day out for me."

You call out Avril's name, but she's never going to hear you with this racket going on, so you get everyone together and all scream,

"AVVVRRRIIIILLLL LE SCREEEAAMMMM!!"

The yell is SO loud, a team of Super Moshis come running to help. They could hear you all the way from the top of Mount Sillimanjaro, where they'd been enlisted to rescue some other monster from a disastrous episode of 'I'm a Celebrity Monster, Get Me Down. Now!' that had just gone a little bit wrong. Apparently, the whole cast had gone on a lunch break three days ago, and forgotten that the Z-list monster was still hanging on a precarious ledge off the north face of the mountain. (Rumours have been circulating that the title of the programme will be changed.)

They help you out of the chamber and explain that there is no use you screaming for Avril, as another team of Super Moshis found her and saved her from the evil clutches of Dr. Strangeglove!

You're a little disappointed that you didn't find Avril yourself, but at least you got to hang out with the Fizzbangs, see some famous pop art and be rescued by the Super Moshis! Not a bad night by all accounts, despite the continuous ringing in your ears that probably won't go away for weeks to come!

THE END

The next day, whilst eating a big bag of Pop Rox, you read *The Daily Growl*'s headline news – it has your picture on it and tells the story about your adventure cracking codes and then saving Avril AND Dustbin! Some of it isn't entirely true, like the part when they say it was you who sang to distract Strangeglove, but it doesn't really matter, as you are branded a hero!

You give up your dreams of Scare Guitar stardom and devote your time to the Super Moshis, with your specialist mission subject being to help out celebrities in distress.

You also decide that you quite like the Haunted House style for your own pad, so head straight out to buy your very own Spider Chandelier. Maybe you'll even get some more Spooky Cobwebs for your next adventure!

You rock, Super Moshi!

THE END

DJ Demonsta plays your request, shouting out, "This one's going out to all you wet monsters out there!"

"Yeeeaaahhh!" the crowd screams back. The 'Monstumble-rella, Rella, Rella' song always gets every monster on the dance floor, with their umbrellas!

Very soon all the umbrellas clear the dance floor (of blue goo foam) and you can see that Avril is not anywhere to be music scene.

What you can see though, are lots of Groanas Brothers posters and they all have lipgloss marks on them. You realize that the marks are obviously just a part of the poster design.

Then you notice a shop selling silver microphones just like Avril's one that Thwack had tripped on earlier! You hadn't been following a track made by Avril, just some Underground Tunnel tourist!

You tell the Fizzbangs your findings and decide to head home.

Back at the Underground Disco, Avril has been safely returned and music is playing again. You'd missed out on all the action, but apparently the Super Moshis had found her.

Despite not finding Avril, you're still very happy that you got to hang out with your favourite band all night, and DJ Demonsta gives you a lifetime's supply of free Fizzbangs' gig tickets – so your life will totally rock from now on anyway!

THE END

"Let's see if she's in here," you say, pointing at the dungeon door.

"Yippee! I can't wait to dust some grooves," cries Dustbin Beaver.

"No time for dancing," you reply, "we're here to find Avril."

You open the door, very slowly, and hear,

"Whoosh!"

Instantly, you are all completely sucked into the dungeon by extremely LOUD music. It leads you straight to the dance floor and you have no choice but to dance.

You try to look for Avril, but soon get very distracted. For some reason, they seem to be playing all of your favourite songs, back-to-back.

One minute you're striking a Lady Goo Goo pose on a platform, the next you're in the thick of the Mosh pit, hair banging and throwing goo around to the Goo Fighters.

"It's better than the Slimelite nightclub in here," you shout over to Thwack.

But Thwack is busy Scare Drumming with his drumsticks, occasionally hitting himself in the head by accident.

You crowd surf your way to the stage and find Dustbin doing his thing on the stage, and the crowd cheering and chanting,

"Dustbin, we love you!"

"We must look for Avril," you say to Dustbin. But

before you know it, you are singing a duet with the floppy haired screamage sensation, and shaking your thang. Then you lead everyone in a dance/jump like you've never jumped before, to Monstro City's number one anthem, guaranteed to get even the most boring monsters dancing, 'Hey Moshi'.

Oh Moshi, you're so fine,
You're so fine you blow my mind.
Hey Moshi! Hey Moshi!
Oh Moshi, you're so fine,
You're so fine you blow my mind,
Hey Moshi!

You soon realize that you are dancing more than the night away, more like your life away! You, Dustbin and the Fizzbangs are caught in a music trap and can't get out, totally lost in music forever!

'Well, at some point Avril will turn up here for a dance,' you think, whilst monster poppin' to 'Catch a Pitch or Try Cryin''. 'But for now these rockin' beats sure beat being a Scare Guitarist.'

THE END

You look very hard at the note, 'there must be something here,' you think, feeling a bit like Detective Whirlock Groans.

```
Xear Readex,
The Fizzbangx - Monsxxocity
Bxnaxa Montana - The Fall
The xroanas Brothxrs - xrowxiwood
Taylor Miffed - Bred to Toast
The Gxo Fighters - Forget to Walk
Dustbin Beaxer - Viva Ixs Moshis
Lady Gooxxo - Peppy-razzi
Pussycax Poppets - Pipe Down
Broccoli Spears - Pepperxizxr
Xairosniff - Poppxt (Looks xike a Furi)
49 Xence - Catch a Pitch or Try Cryin'
Xxxxx Xx ........ Xxxxxx!
```

"There must be something about all those missing letters," you say. You start writing down all the missing letters to fill in the gaps.

d - r - s - t - r - a - n - g - e - g - l - o - v - e   g - o - t - m - e - h - e - l - p - a - v - r -i - l - l- e."

Suddenly, you realize that the missing letters must be a code, "Dr. Strangeglove got me, help Avril Le . . . Scream!"

"Nice work, Moshi!" says the Elder, leader of the Super Moshis.

"Thanks," you reply, quite pleased. "But if Dr. Strangeglove took Avril from backstage, how would she have had time to write a note?"

"We have heard from HQ," begins another Super Moshi, "that Dr. Strangeglove was last seen by some Zommer one-eyed witnesses, heading towards the Haunted House. Let's head there now!"

"Have you forgotten about the glittery footprints?" says DJ Demonsta, mixing up the situation perfectly, like only really good DJs can.

Your instinct tells you that paw prints are often great clues, but if Strangeglove has been seen making his way to the haunted house, maybe you should go there?

'Roly Poly mackerel! Another decision to make!' you think to yourself, not really sure why fish is on your brain, perhaps you're just getting a little peckish?

If you decide to ignore the one-eyed witness account, and follow your instinct that Avril would not have had time to write the note, **turn to page 35.** You were the one who cracked the code after all!

If you decide to head to take the Super Moshis' advice and head to the haunted house, **turn to page 63.**

You jump on the Gift Island Ferry, and your evening trip to Rockstar Reef begins.

"Welcome aboard!" cheers the ferry captain monster, covered head to toe in this year's sailor wear. "Tonight, my dear monster, you're in for one monstar-licious adventure!"

'I wonder what the captain means by adventure?' you think. 'I thought we were just heading to Rockstar Reef?'

"Thank you!" you reply, letting the captain's comment slide.

As you pass the *CloudyCloth Clipper*, you shout out, "Ahoy, there!" You can see all the monsters still queuing up to board, while you race along the waves. You're bound to get to Rockstar Reef first, have plenty of time to practise, and then monster smash the others out of the competition with your Scare Guitar genius.

'Result!' you think.

Soon, the crowd of monsters and Monstro City are just a dot on the horizon and you are far out at sea.

"Where are we?" you ask the captain, just a little worried that you can't see anything but the stars.

"We're heading towards the 1, 2, 3 Cook! Islands, for a spot of dinner," explains the captain.

"But I want to go to Rockstar Reef," you reply.

"Oh, yes, we shall be going there," replies the captain, "but you'll need food first."

You and the captain dine on a feast fit for the stars.

'Appropriate,' you think, 'seeing as I'll be a Scare Guitar star very soon.'

Sitting on a star picnic rug, you gobble up mounds of extremely rare and unusual Snails Legs, followed by Starlight Cookies, and wash everything down with crystal glasses full of Sparkling Champoo – an acquired taste.

You get back on-board the Ferry, and the captain shows you how to stargaze using a telescope.

"There's Monster Major," the captain cries, showing you a lovely collection of sparkling stars in the shape of a strange, rather ugly-looking monster. "And that's Monster Miner."

Monstargazing is lots of fun, but you begin to wonder if you will ever make it to Rockstar Reef! **Turn to page 55.**

You leave the piece of paper on the Vanity Table and tell the Super Moshis you're going to follow the glittery paw prints. The note is surely just a list of Avril's favourite songs?

"Okay," says the leader of the Super Moshis, "we'll take a look at the note, while you follow the trail."

You walk very slowly along the glittery trail. It's hard to see in the emergency lighting, so Riff pulls out a Tentacle Torch from his pocket.

"Why do you have a Tentacle Torch on you?" you ask curiously.

"I use it as a pretend microphone in front of the mirror," replies Riff. "Avril's not the only singer in the Fizzbangs band you know."

"Aha," you reply. You find it reassuring to think that even rockstars are normal monsters at heart.

Now that you can see properly, you all walk a lot faster. The paw prints lead you all around the dressing room in a series of lots and lots of circles.

"Look at the crazy circles of paw print patterns on the floor," you say, a little dizzy from running round and round.

"Grumble, grumble!"

"What was that?" asks DJ Demonsta.

"Nothing," you reply, knowing full well that it's nothing sinister, just your stomach growling. You haven't had anything to eat since your Eye Pie breakfast, and you're really hungry!

Eventually, the paw prints take you to the side of the stage, where, in a dark corner, you see a sleeping monster.

"Zzzzzz!"

'Avril can't have been here all along, can she?' you wonder to yourself. But then Riff points his torch into the dark corner . . .

"Dustbin!" you cry, only just remembering that you hadn't seen him for quite some time. "The paw prints are yours?" you ask, waking him up.

"Oh, those, err," he replies, yawning, "yes, well I had a little bit of an accident. I decided to paint my toenails with glittery nail polish, but I ended up painting my whole feet. I was a bit embarrassed, so I ran away to hide and I must've fallen asleep!"

"Oh dear," you sigh, realizing you have been on a wild Beaver chase! "We thought your glittery paw prints were something to do with Avril going missing!"

"That's it!" you hear one of the Super Moshis shout from Avril's dressing room.

You, Dustbin and the Fizzbangs race back to see them.

"What is it?" you ask.

"We've cracked the code!" they cheer.

They explain that all the letter xs are covering up letters;

"d – r – s – t – r – a – n – g – e – g – l – o – v – e g – o – t – m – e – h – e – l – p – a – v – r – i – l – l – e – s – c – r – e – a – m.'

"Tamara Tesla eat your heart out!" cries DJ Demonsta. "That's very impressive. But er, what does that long line of letters actually mean?"

"Dr. Strangeglove got me, help Avril Le Scream!" you say. You're quite a puzzle wizard yourself and just wish you'd taken a look at it in the first place.

"Nice work!" says the Super Moshi congratulating you. "Our latest report from Super Moshi HQ is that Dr. Strangeglove was last seen inside the Ice-Scream shop on Ooh La Lane."

"We're heading there now," says another Super Moshi. "Are you in?"

If you decide to go to the Ice-Scream shop with the Super Moshis, **turn to page 49.** You want in on the action!

If you decide to let the Super Moshis head to the Ice-Scream shop alone, **turn to page 41.** You need dinner before dessert, and it's always best to leave these things to the experts.

Leaving the Super Moshis to do their own super things, you, the Fizzbangs and Dustbin Beaver keep searching for more clues as to where Avril might have gone to look for her voice.

You stare at the pop art painting blankly, and think carefully.

'If I was looking for my voice, where would I look first?' you wonder to yourself. 'Hmm, I'd probably leave it somewhere safe and sound.'

"Are there any safe places around here?" you ask anyone who's listening.

"Not really," replies Riff, (he's been a bit quiet for a while, as he had yet another saw finger, poor darling). "Everywhere down here feels a little scary to me." Sawfinger acted all tough, but really he was a little sweetie Zommer at heart.

"What about the barred prison, where Cry Baby is? That's a safe place," suggests Dustbin. "It's a bit of a dump in there though, even if I do say so myself. I said I would never go there, but as monsters like to say, Never say Never . . . Lad dad a da dee."

And Dustbin drifts off into a rendition of another of his songs.

Just then, DJ Demonsta spins around and has a brainwave, or it could be just a wave of light from the fizzy fireworks popping out of his volcanic head, you're not sure.

He doesn't say anything, so you think that probably your second thought is correct.

"This is useless," you say, then suddenly seeing something etched in the wall of the fifth tunnel along. You look at it more closely and it says,

'Avril was here!'

"Let's head this way," you suggest, pointing down the fifth tunnel along. "I have a good feeling about it!"

You get about halfway down the tunnel when you hear, **"ARRRGGGHHHH!"** as a nearby door is opened.

"What was that?" you ask, surprised, shocked, astonished AND stunned! "I pretty much jumped out of my skin!"

"Oh, that's just the Chamber of Screams," explains Missi Tinkles, "they're always screaming in there, that lot. It's where monsters go to let off scream, swap screams and go get a brand new scream, when you've lost your own."

"Oh, okay," you reply, not really paying enough attention to what you're hearing.

"BOOOM, Shhh, BOOM, Shhh!" you hear as another nearby door is opened.

"What was that?" you ask, once again feeling every form of alarm,

"Oh, that's just the House of Rock," explains DJ Demonsta. "If you want to find your rockstar yelling voice, you can go there."

"Oh, okay," you reply, not really listening very well again.

And FINALLY it dawns on you. Avril could be in

either of those places trying to find her rocking Le Scream!

But was her voice a scream or a rockstar yell? It's hard to tell the difference these days. But you need to find Avril and fast, so you have to make a decision quickly. What will it be this time, Moshi? Which door will you walk through? And will it be the one to Avril's monstardom?

If you decide that you should head to the Chamber of Screams, **turn to page 17.**

If you decide to rock up at the House of Rock, **turn to page 58.**

'There's nothing I can do about a smoke signal,' you think to yourself. "It's probably just Dizzy making changes at the En-Gen Station."

So you and the captain dock the Gift Island Ferry in the super swanky Rockstar Reef Rockstar Dock, ready to search for some rocking civilization.

"At last," you sigh. "I shall be the Scare Guitarist champion!"

Just as you get ready to jump onto the pier, you hear a loud drum roll,

"Pat-a-pat-a, pat-a-pat-a, pat-a-pat-a, pat-a . . ." the drum roll puts you off, and your legs begin to wobble and wobble and . . . yikes! You fall in between the ferry and the pier. "SPLASH!"

"Ouch!" you cry out, using all your strength to climb back up, "What is that noise?"

"Every time someone arrives at Rockstar Reef, they are greeted with a rocking drum roll," explains the captain, helping you back on to your feet. The captain has clearly visited the Reef before.

The pier is covered with a luscious red carpet, nothing like your Scruffy Carpet Floor at home. You feel like a famous celebrity heading to the Monster Me rock awards, and wish you weren't soaking wet after your fall in the water.

The captain suggests you do a whirlwind tour of the island, and like all good tourists you make your first stop on the Reef the Rocking Souvenir Shop. You buy a Rock

Clock for your house and a Rockin' Rocking Chair, and get it all delivered to rock up at your house some time soon. You also pick out The Lil Rocking Guitar, for all your little Moshlings to rock on.

After a spot of rocking shopping, you head to Monsieur Three Swords to see crayon wax versions of all your favourite stars, 49 Pence, The Goo Fighters, Hairosniff, Broccoli Spears (ahem) and . . . The Fizzbangs.

"Oh dear," you sigh, seeing the colourful waxy version of Avril Le Scream. You remember back to earlier on when you were looking forward to seeing her outrageous yelling self at The Underground Disco.

The captain, looks at you strangely, and as you look back you see that the wax model of Avril bears a spookily striking resemblance to the ferry captain.'How odd,' you think to yourself. 'I must be seeing things now!'

Turn to page 66.

Ignoring the Super Moshis' information about the whereabouts of Dr. Strangeglove, you and the Fizzbangs begin to follow the sparkly paw prints around the Underground Disco.

You walk very slowly along the glittery trail. It's hard to see in the emergency lighting, so Riff pulls out a Tentacle Torch from his pocket.

"Why do you have a Tentacle Torch on you?" you ask curiously.

"I use it as a pretend microphone in front of the mirror," replies Riff. "Avril's not the only singer in the Fizzbangs band you know."

"Aha," you reply. You find it reassuring to think that even rockstars are normal monsters at heart, just looking for their next break.

Now that you can see properly, you all walk a lot faster. The paw prints lead you all around the dressing room in a series of lots and lots of circles.

"Whoever left these prints must have been in quite a panic, just look at the crazy circles of paw prints on the floor," you say, a little dizzy from running round and round following the prints.

"If I'd just seen Dr. Strangeglove, I'd be panicking!" cries Missi Tinkles.

'She's right,' you think to yourself, trying to think about what Dr. Strangeglove would want from Avril anyway.

"Grumble, grumble!"

"What was that?" asks DJ Demonsta.

"Nothing," you reply, knowing full well that it's nothing sinister, just your stomach growling. You haven't had anything to eat since your Eye Pie breakfast, and you're really hungry!

Eventually the paw prints take you to the side of the stage, where, in a really dark corner, you see a sleeping monster.

"Zzzzzz!"

'Avril can't have been here all along, can she?' you wonder to yourself. But then Riff points his torch into the dark corner . . .

"Dustbin!" you cry, only just remembering that you hadn't seen him for quite some time. "The paw prints are yours?" you ask, waking him up.

"Oh, those, err," he replies, yawning. "Yes, well I had a little bit of an accident. While you were reading that note, I decided to paint my toenails with glittery nail polish, but I ended up painting my whole feet. I was a bit embarrassed, so I ran away to hide and I must've fallen asleep!"

"Oh dear," you sigh, realizing you have been on a wild Beaver chase! "We thought your glittery paw prints were something to do with Avril going missing!"

"Well, I'm not sure if there is anything more we can do now," you say to the gang. "There aren't any more clues, and it's getting late. Besides, I don't know about you but I really need something to eat."

Or is there something you can do? **Turn to page 42** to find out.

You head towards the Groanas Brothers' poster, take a closer look and give it a good sniff.

"Yep, that's definitely Glueberry lipgloss," you say. "We must be following in Avril's paw steps, all right."

You turn around to speak to everyone about what to do next and notice someone's missing.

"Where's Dustbin?" you ask.

"He's Runaway Over There, Love," says Riff, pointing towards the dancing dungeon, and laughing at his reference to Dustbin's latest hit!

"Oh well, another one loses the Dust, I suppose," you reply.

You start walking again, feeling like you're definitely on the right track, when suddenly you are at a dead end.

"Now what?" asks Thwack, thwacking his head against the wall.

Just as you're beginning to think that Dustbin had the right idea going into the Dancing Dungeon and you think of turning back, you look down at the floor, and notice two lights at the end of the tunnel! They're both glowing disco lights. One is luminous pink and the other cool blue.

Which one do you pick up? Which one do you think Avril chose?

If you pick up the luminous pink disco light, **turn to page 70.** Pink has to be Avril's favourite colour right?

If you pick up the cool blue disco light, **turn to page 61.** Avril was feeling pretty blue, and she's always been too cool for school.

You race towards the Super Moshis, leaving the Fizzbangs and Dustbin Beaver behind, desperately trying to decide which way to turn.

You want to hang out with your favourite rock band and pop's number one floppy-haired heart-throb, but you're much more likely to find Avril, and save the day, by joining the Super Moshis.

Running faster than you have ever run before, you eventually catch up with the caped and masked monster crew.

"Can . . . puff, puff . . . I join . . . puff, puff . . . you?" you pant.

"Of course you can," replies the leader of the team, passing you your very own shiny red cape and mask.

"Wow!" you gasp, excitedly putting them on and trying to walk along at the same time.

The Super Moshis tell you to listen up, and explain that their mission, should you wish to join them, is to find Avril Le Scream, bring her back to the Underground Disco and save Monstro City's music industry.

It all sounds so exciting! You're more than happy to join the monster mission and help find Avril.

The Super Moshis hear that Avril was last seen looking for her voice in the Underground Music Tunnels, but the Super Moshi HQ is reporting that the evil genius, Dr. Strangeglove, has captured her and taken her above ground. The Super Moshis realize that Strangeglove must have monster-napped Avril, knowing that they would come looking for her.

"He must want to trap US!" they cry.

But the caped super stars decide that they and you (!) have the power to outsmart Strangeglove, so the mission should still go ahead.

"Our first task is to find a way out of these tunnels and get back up there," they tell you, "and then we can work out what to do next."

You quickly realize that you can help the Super Moshis with their first conundrum.

Being a little worried about getting home, you had dropped a trail of Pop Rox along your journey so far. So, you suggest you follow the trail of Rox back to The Underground Disco, and get above ground from there.

"Fantastic idea, Moshi!" cheers the Super Moshi leader.

The team turn around and follow you along your trail, back to the Disco. You pass the Fizzbangs and Dustbin on the way, still staring at the graffiti and deciding which way to go. Zooming past, you wave and they all look up and wave back, (Dustbin just flicks his hair) amazed to see the Super Moshis following you!

Back at the Underground Disco, you find a note in Avril's dressing room with a code on it. You and the Super Moshis quickly crack the code and it leads you to the Ice-Scream Shop on Ooh La Lane.

"Let's go!"

At the Ice-Scream Shop, you find Giuseppe Gelato, the

Ice Scream man, tied up in a corner and unable to serve any Ice Scream. You serve a couple of the customers screaming for their Ice Scream NOW, while the Super Moshis search the place for signs of Strangeglove and Avril.

Just as you are serving a mud cone full of glueberry sorbet, spaghetti sauce and chocolate lip sprinkles, you hear an evil laugh and a strange noise:

"Mwah, ha, ha! . . . Ooh, ouch!"

It's coming from the giant freezer out the back, so you give the customer the Ice Scream half finished and head out there to see what's going on.

While you were busy serving sundaes, the Super Moshis have found Avril. The strange noise you heard was Strangeglove!

"Just in time!" shouts the leader of the Super Moshis. He passes Avril over to you, while he and the rest of his team chase off Strangeglove.

The next day, Avril is reunited with the rest of the Fizzbangs, who, after getting completely lost in the Underground Music Tunnels, had to be saved by another team of Super Moshis themselves!

You may not have seen the Fizzbangs perform, or taken part in the Scare Guitar auditions, but you've made some super-duper Super Moshi friends from your adventure! You're now going to devote your time to spreading the word about the Super Moshis, and also a spot of Ice Scream making on the side, from time-to-time. You go Super Ice Scream Moshi!

THE END

The next day, *The Daily Growl*'s headline is 'Le Ice Scream Sensation!' Roary reports that the Super Moshis had found Avril in the Ice-Scream Shop with Dr. Strangeglove. They had saved her and had all been awarded Super Moshi hero awards – the biggest Ice Screams you have ever seen!

You're really pleased that Avril was found, and that you managed to get home for a spot of dinner, you were completely monstarving! But you can't help feeling a little disappointed that you weren't part of the team who tracked her down, even though you had been the one to crack the code, and more than anything that you missed out on the biggest Ice Screams ever!

"Oh, well," you tell everyone you know, "at least I've got tickets to the next Fizzbangs' concert, and I've got plenty of time to practise for next year's Scare Guitar auditions!"

THE END

But no, there is nothing more you can do, so you don't! The Super Moshis have already left with the note and there are no other leads to Avril's whereabouts whatsoever.

The next day, *The Daily Growl* reports that the Super Moshis had found Avril at the Haunted House with Dr. Strangeglove. You read all about how they had saved her and all been awarded Super Moshi hero awards. Strangeglove's evil plans were thwarted and he had been outsmarted by the Super Moshis once again.

"That could have been me!" you cry.

You're really pleased that Avril was found, and that you managed to get home for a spot of dinner, you were completely monstarving! But you also can't help feeling a little disappointed that you weren't part of the team who tracked her down, especially as you were the one who cracked the code in the letter. You'll probably never know how Avril ever had time to write that note in the first place.

"Oh, well," you tell everyone you know, "at least I've got tickets to the next Fizzbangs' concert, and I've got plenty of time to practise for next year's Scare Guitar auditions."

Secretly, you vow to sign up and help out on the next Super Moshi mission, you'd much rather do that than play the Scare Guitar any day!

THE END

Left it is!

You lead the celebrity gang to the left, and the music gets louder and louder. You're not quite sure what it is, as it sounds like a monster mash-up of everything from the latest Lady Goo Goo track, 'Peppy-razzi', to the classic Hairosniff tune, 'Poppet (Looks like a Furi)'.

You're busy trying to work out what the song is, when suddenly you hear, "Thwack!" as Thwack thwacks onto the floor.

"Ouch!" he shouts, rubbing his Furi knee.

"What did you fall over?" you ask.

Thwack looks down and picks up what looks like a shiny silver Ice Scream cone.

"Ooh, yummy, Ice Scream," he smiles, about to eat it.

"Pause!" yells DJ Demonsta in total DJ mode. "Rewind back to a few hours ago, Thwack. We are looking for Avril and that, my dear Furi, is Avril's microphone!"

"Den, den, den," plays Missi Tinkles on her piano for dramatic effect. "It's a clue!"

"Avril must have come this way!" you cheer, realizing you must've picked the right path. "Let's pick up the pace and find out where she's got to."

Thwack beats his drumsticks on the walls, creating a thumping tune that you can all walk to.

Missi Tinkles plays a few notes on her piano and the whole gang walks in time to the beat, 5, 6, 7, 8 . . . step, spin on the spot, step, clap your paws, step, spin on the spot, step, clap your paws. You feel the rhythm and all make up your own dance moves as you walk.

You're busy walking like a prehistoric monster when you see a sign on a dungeon door.

'Come in and dance the night away . . .' it says.

'Ooh, how tempting,' you think to yourself.

Just then, Riff notices something shiny on the wall up ahead. It's a poster of the Groanas Brothers with a lipgloss lip print in the middle of it.

On closer inspection, Missi Tinkles notices that the gloss is glueberry colour and flavour. "It could be Avril's," says Missi Tinkles.

"But Avril also loves to dance," Dr Demonsta adds into the mix. "She might be behind that door, dancing the night away."

"What do you think?" everyone asks you.

So, what do you think you should all do? The choice is yours!

If you decide to dance the night away, **turn to page 21.**

If you decide to walk in the direction of the poster, **turn to page 37.**

It seems a shame to leave Rockstar Reef so soon, but someone needs your help.

"Let's head starboard towards the signal, Captain!" you cry out.

The captain turns the ferry around, and you wave goodbye to the reef that may have held your destiny, "Goodbye!"

Racing towards the signal, you peer up at the sky and realize that the stars are leading the way. You'd heard that sailors follow the stars, but this is ridiculous. The stars are actually forming arrows and beckoning you forwards.

'I could soooo be a sailor,' you think.

As you get closer and closer to the smoke, you realize that you are getting close to Monstro City – back where you started your sea adventure!

At first, the smoke signal is so dense you can't actually see anyone or anything, but as it begins to clear a little bit, you see hundreds of monsters scrabbling around on a boat and frantically doggy-paddling in the water. The last time you saw that many monsters was . . . at the Underground Disco, waiting for the Fizzbangs to perform . . . then you realize . . .

"It's the Scare Guitarists on the *CloudyCloth Clipper*!" you gasp.

"It looks more like it was the *CloudyCloth Dipper*!" replies the captain. "Let's help them aboard the ferry and our lifeboats."

So you and the captain set to work saving the entire, very enormous crew of the *Cloudy Cloth*, including poor old Cap'n Buck, who seems more than a little bit upset about his shoe for some reason.

"Me boot!" he is crying out. "Me boot!"

With a ferry and three lifeboats full of wannabee Scare Guitarists, a slightly soggy Simon Growl and a tearful Cap'n Buck, still crying out for his boot, you head to the shore. Which is actually right there anyway, as it seems the *Cloudy Cloth* hadn't actually left The Port yet!

'Silly smoking signal!' you think to yourself, realizing the whole rescue had been a little bit pointless, as the water was just an inch deep and no one had in fact been drowning! 'What a rubbish night! I didn't get to see the Fizzbangs, I never made it to Rockstar Reef and I didn't get to win the Scare Guitar competition . . .'

Turn to page 15.

As none of the Fizzbangs seem to have any idea where Avril might be, and Dustbin Beaver is too busy posing and singing, you decide to take charge of the situation and get some experts on the case.

"I'm going to the Volcano to ask the Super Moshis for help," you suggest. "Who's in?"

You hear choruses of 'Me', 'Me, me, me' and a few 'so, fa, la, te, dos' too, and you and the entire musical gang find your way out of the Underground Disco chambers, following the emergency glow-worm lighting.

When you surface above ground, you find yourselves on Sludge Street, outside a rather battered looking shed and an old empty building.

Walking along, you head across and over the Monstro City hills, pass the Puzzle Palace and up towards the steaming Volcano.

Carefully jumping across the lava moat, you try to enter the Super Moshi headquarters, but that's when you find out that you need your Moshi Passport to enter, and you've left yours at home!

"You cannot enter without a members' passport," says the Gatekeeper.

"Oh no!" you gasp.

The Gatekeeper sees who you are with.

"Dustbin!" he cries, "I'm your biggest fan!"

"Really?" you say, but then you realize that you can totally use this fan devotion to your advantage.

You start to explain, "Dustbin needs to speak to the Super Moshis, the Gatekeeper . . ."

"Do I?" asks Dustbin, "I thought you were the one . . ."

"Shhh," you shush Dustbin and continue. "What's your favourite Beaver tune, Gatekeeper?"

"Well," begins the Gatekeeper, "I think it has to be Do the Dustbin!"

"That's not one of my . . ." begins Dustbin.

"Shhh. Just sing it!" you interrupt.

So Dustbin begins to sing a completely made up tune, (little do you all know, it will be his next big hit!) and it completely distracts the Gatekeeper. Meanwhile, you and the Fizzbangs secretly enter the Volcano.

Inside the Volcano, you see the giant screens in front of you, "How exciting!" you cry. "I want to be a Super Moshi!"

DJ Demonsta explains the missing Avril situation to the Elder Furi and a top team of Super Moshis, while you marvel at all the flashing lights and swirling Rox, "Wow!"

The Super Moshis are happy to make finding Avril their latest mission and ask you all whether you want to go along too.

If you decide not to choose the mission, leaving it up to the Super Moshis, **turn to page 10.** You'd rather stay safe and sound inside the Volcano, and let the experts do their stuff.

If you decide to help the Super Moshis find Avril by becoming one yourself, **turn to page 68.**

You, a glittery Dustbin Beaver, the Fizzbangs and the Super Moshis, head to the Ice-Scream Shop on Ooh La Lane.

The shop is a total mess of Ice Scream, cones, wafers, sprinkles and sauces in more revolting flavours than you have ever ice-dreamed of!

After eating your fill, you, the Fizzbangs and the Super Moshis eventually find Dr. Strangeglove at the back of the shop in the enormous freezer.

"I was wondering when you might turn up!" he shivers.

"You were expecting us?" asks Thwack, hitting himself on the head with his drumsticks.

"I wrote you that note, didn't I?" replies Dr. Strangeglove.

"You wrote a note?" asks Missi Tinkles. "Can I play it?" But she soon realizes he means the piece of paper and not a key for her to play on her keyboard. Sometimes Missi Tinkles gets a little too lost in music.

"I wrote the note to see if I could lure you all into my trap!" explains Strangeglove. "I knew that if I took Avril, the Super Moshis would come for her and I was right! Now I can trap you all in my giant freezer, freezing the Super Moshis forever!"

'It all makes sense, now,' you think. 'I knew there was no way Avril could have written that note.'

"Where's Avril Le Scream?" you ask.

"With all the other Screams! Ha, ha, ha!" replies Strangeglove.

You stop to think for a fraction of a second, and realize that he doesn't mean your stomach, but in a tub!

You scan the room, there are hundreds of tubs, but most of them are far too small for Avril to be inside. You spy a larger one, but it's right behind Strangeglove. How are you going to get to it?

Then it dawns on you – you have eaten so much Ice Scream and you are freezing cold, making your stomach feel solid as a rock. You roll yourself into a ball and fling yourself at the Ice Scream tubs. One by one, the tubs fall down like dominos, and eventually reach the giant tub behind Strangeglove. The force of all the tubs together, knocks the giant tub over. Avril comes rolling out straight towards you and away from Strangeglove.

The Super Moshis grab Avril and you all race out of the Ice-Scream Shop. Dr. Strangeglove is frozen in shock and from being in the freezer so long! Eventually, he snaps out of it and scarpers off.

The next day, you and the Super Moshis celebrate finding Avril together. You abandon your Scare Guitar Dreams for a life devoted to the Super Moshis – oh and also to eating as much Ice Scream as possible!

THE END

You make your excuses to the remaining Fizzbang band members, acknowledge Dustbin Beaver with a flick of your fur, and skedaddle, as fast as you can. You sing Any dream will do! at the top of your voice as you go to The Port to follow your dreams.

Using the small amount of glow from the emergency lighting powered by lots of jars of Glowbugs, you feel your way along the hallways, out of the Underground Disco and into the underground alleyway.

The Peppy-razzi are there taking photos, so you do your duty and strike a pose or two, or three, with your Scare Guitar, before you head off. You never know, you could be the next Scare Guitarist superstar, and if so, they'd need lots of pictures of you on the road to monstardom!

Passing scary bats, Cry Baby and some new work from Art Lee, Monstro City's amateur graffiti artist and the next Danksy, you keep your eyes peeled for a way out. But for some reason you just can't see the light.

You reach a knife and fork in the road and decide to turn left, as you can see some figures in the distance.

'That must be where everyone went,' you think.

You head towards the shadows and find a rope ladder leading to the light. You climb up and find yourself back above ground on Main Street.

"Phew!" you sigh, relieved and a little out of breath, "I've made it!"

But you haven't made it. You're only halfway there. Now you have to get from Main to The Port.

You race along the street and see the sign to The Port. Jumping a barrier you creak your way over a rickety old bridge and find yourself . . .

. . . At The Port of course! You followed the sign didn't you?!

You pop into Babs' Boutique to pick up a souvenir Scare Bear (the one that looks like a rockstar). You know that you don't have much time, but you want to always remember the day you became famous.

Then, you spy hoards of monsters climbing on-board the *CloudyCloth Clipper*.

"I'm never gonna get on," you sigh, "there are far too many monsters for that boat."

You're just about to give up when you spot the Gift Island Ferry with a little sign, almost hidden from sight, right by it.

'Evening cruise to Rockstar Reef for one night only, and for one monster only.'

You weigh up your options. You could queue up for the *CloudyCloth* that's what you've been told to do after all, or you could get your own little boat and try to make it to the Reef faster?

If you decide to join the rest of the Scare Guitarists on board the *CloudyCloth Clipper*, **turn to page 12.**

If you try to board the Gift Island Ferry, **turn to page 25.**

You and the captain head for the Hard Sock Café.

When you arrive, it's heaving with monstar-celebrities, playing real guitars, not Scare Guitars, and jamming together. It's awesome!

No one has heard about the audition and they are too busy talking about themselves to notice you. But you don't really mind, the music is rocking, and you love being surrounded by rockstar celebs.

"I'm gonna stay here forever!" you sing at the top of your voice. "I'm gonna learn how to sing!"

You turn to see the Captain on the stage singing away. You'd always thought the captain was a sly monster, with hidden talents. You listen and hear that the Captain has the voice of an Angel SkyPony Moshling, the voice of a star, the voice of . . . Avril Le Scream!

"That's it!" you gasp, loud enough to be heard over all the singing, strumming, and thwacking. "The captain is Avril Le Scream in disguise!"

You can't believe you hadn't realized sooner. She must have used her disguise to escape The Underground Disco, hide from her adoring fans and come on holiday to Rockstar Reef to get away from it all. She'd probably wanted to go underground, but saw a way out when everyone left.

'Good on her,' you think. 'The life of a star sure is tough.'

Lying on your hammock later on, you stare up at the

celebrity stars, (special stars that only twinkle over the exclusive Rockstar Reef), and think to yourself, 'This, my fans . . . is where I belong. This is my song."

Maybe one day you'll even learn how to play a proper guitar to strum along to your song!

THE END

You finish monstargazing and your mind starts drifting off. You begin to fall slowly, but surely . . . asleep **. . . zzzzz . . .**

"Right then!"

You immediately wake, with a start, as the captain explains the next part of the adventure.

Little did you know, but part of the Rockstar Reef evening trip on the ferry includes a night-time water ski!

You remember back to the captain's words, when you first jumped aboard, "Tonight, my dear monster, you're in for one monstar-licious adventure!" Now it was all beginning to make sense. You are on some sort of night-time tourist cruise of the islands around Monstro City! Rockstar Reef is purely a stop-off on the trip. At this rate you'll never make it to the Scare Guitar audition in time. How can you have been so foolish?

'Oh, well,' you sigh to yourself. 'I'm here now, I suppose.'

The captain gets the water-skiing gear together and shows you what to do. You're not really listening, as you've been skiing before. You're a little full from dinner, but you've always loved to ski, more on the slopes of the Frosty Pop Glacier, but snow, water, all the same thing, right . . . ?

. . . Wrong! They may be made of the same thing, but the waves of Potion Ocean are NOT like the lovely powdery snow of the CharChar slopes. With water spraying up all around you, you toss and turn on your skis, like you're having one bad nightmare after another, over one wave after another, and another. You grab on for dear life and try desperately to hold on to your dinner for dear life too!

"This was not a good idea!" you scream, but no one can hear you through the crashing of the waves and the sound of the rushing water behind you.

"Bleeeuuuurgggh!"

What a waste of all that monstar-licious food.

The ferry whizzes round in a circle one last time, just so you have time to lose the rest of your dinner, "Bleurggh!" and slows down for you to be reeled back on board.

"Now, wasn't that fun?" asks the captain, as you scramble aboard, feeling more than a little scrambled yourself. And by this you mean actually physically like a scrambled egg, not that you would like one. Food is pretty far from your mind right now!

You hear a bird burping and you realize there was one seagull that had gotten very lucky that night, dining on your gourmet barf! Nice!

The captain calms you down and you head off across the ocean.

Finally, you reach Rockstar Reef. But, just as the captain lets down the anchor, you see a luminous smoke signal in the distance, shining through the black sky like a giant glow-worm with wind.

"Who is it?" you ask the captain.

The captain uses a telescope, but can't quite see who it is, just that the signal is coming from the direction of Monstro City.

"Shall we go back to help?" the captain asks you.

The choice is yours, what do you do?

If you ignore the luminous smoke signal, **turn to page 33.** How would you be of any help, since you couldn't even keep your own dinner down? Besides, you have finally made it to Rockstar Reef, you can't turn back now.

If you decide to head towards the smoke signal, to see if there is anything you can do to help, **turn to page 45.**

You, the Fizzbangs and Dustbin, rock on up to the House of Rock and rock on the door three times.

"Rock on!" you hear the Door Monster scream, and the door opens letting you in. "Welcome rockers! You ready to rock around the clock?"

"Well, actually we're here to find Avril Le Scream," you explain, but the Door Monster is too busy head banging the table in time to the music to hear you.

The room is full of, well mainly just rocks and more rocks, and a giant clock in the middle of the Mosh pit.

'That must be for rocking around the clock,' you think.

"This place rocks! It's so much better than the Hard Sock Café!" cheers Thwack, beating his drumsticks on anything and everything that makes a sound, as he walks this way and that.

"We're leaving no rock unturned, until we find Avril," you declare. There's a lot of rocks there, so it's going to take you quite some time!

After turning over about a hundred rocks and still not finding Avril, you take a break for a quick Toad Soda.

You spy a group of Super Moshis celebrating in the corner of the room. You go over and ask them what the good news is.

"We found Avril Le Scream," they say in unison.

"Oh," you reply and you're not sure how you feel. Very happy that Avril has been found of course, but a little disappointed that you weren't the one to find her.

"Where did you find her?" you ask.

"At the Ice-Scream Shop," they reply, "with Dr. Strangeglove!"

You call over the Fizzbangs and Dustbin and tell them the news, then you all head back to the Underground Disco to reunite the band. Along the way you find Axl Van Slap, who, realizing that a one-monster band wasn't working for him, chokes on his pride and joins you.

Together with Avril, who found her voice (she'd left it in her bathroom sink) the Fizzbangs have their best performance yet! What's more, because the entire audience is still at the Scare Guitar auditions, you and Dustbin are the only people watching.

"A private performance – how cool!" And all the songs are dedicated to you!

"You Rox!" you cheer at the top of your voice.

And the entire band look right at you and sing, "We know!"

Listening to the Fizzbangs on your Frypod the next day you sing yourself to sleep, "I just can't get that rocking music outta my head!"

THE END

After unsuccessfully searching The Underground Disco for signs of Avril, you, the remaining Fizzbang band members and Dustbin Beaver, huddle up and discuss what to do next.

"When you last saw Avril, what did she say?" you ask. "Anything unusual?"

"She did mention something about wanting the band to go underground," cries Missi Tinkles, fluttering her Luvli eyelashes. "Oh, and that she was very nearly out of Glueberry Lipgloss."

"But she wouldn't leave without telling us, would she?" says Thwack, twirling his drumsticks in his big Furi hands. "Especially not when we were supposed to be on stage."

"It's like a runaway love," sings Dustbin Beaver, which doesn't help the situation one little bit. "Aveeeeril, Aveeeeril!"

'Maybe, she has gone to the underground music scene,' you think, trying to block out the noise coming from Dustbin Beaver. (You love music but there's a time and a place for ballads!) 'Either that or someone has taken Avril. Maybe the Super Moshis could help out?'

If you think Avril must have gone to the underground music tunnels and want to go in search for her, **turn to page 13.**

If you think the best plan is to first enlist the help of the Super Moshis, **turn to page 47.**

Picking up the cool blue lantern, Missi Tinkles screams out, "Good choice! Blue is Avril's favourite colour!"

"Phew!" you sigh, relieved. Suddenly the whole underground chamber is magically transformed into a giant music hall, full of blue goo foam! It's absolutely positively foamazing!

"Woohoo, a blue goo foam party!" cheers Thwack. "I've always wanted to go to one of these."

"So has Avril," calls Missi Tinkles over the loud music, "she must be here somewhere."

You and the Fizzbangs search through the foam trying to find Avril. Hunting high and low, suddenly you hear, "Ah ha!"

It's DJ Demonsta and it looks likes he's found something, how exciting!

"The decks!" he cries, happily getting ready to scratch some records.

Your heart sinks, and you wonder if you're ever going to find Avril. More and more blue goo foam is being pumped into the room every minute. What with that, the wet ice spray, and 'It's Raining Monsters', and the 'Gloop, Gloop Song' pumping out of the speakers, you and the rest of the Fizzbangs are soaked and sliding away.

You battle through the foamy oceans, sail the seven foams, and leave absolutely no foam unturned! But still you can't find Avril. What are you going to do next?

If you ask DJ Demonsta to play the 'Monstumble-rella, Rella, Rella', song to try to combat some of the foam, so you can see more clearly, **turn to page 20.**

If you give up the foamy cause and try to find a way out, **turn to page 73.**

You, the Fizzbangs and the Super Moshis head to the Haunted House. On the way out, you find Dustbin Beaver asleep in a corner, covered in glitter! You wake him up.

"The glittery paw prints were yours!" you cry.

"Oh, errr, I," begins Dustbin.

"Well, we're off to the Haunted House," you explain, and ask him to come with you. He might be useful for something later on. You realize how lucky you were to follow the clues in the letter, rather than the glittery footprints!

You traverse the streets of Monstro City, finally arriving at the crooked gates of the Haunted House.

"It's like 'Bats on my Mind' by The Vanted round here!" you joke nervously, trying to impress the Fizzbangs with your musical knowledge and laugh rather than cry tears of fears at the same time. But it's not really a time for jokes, so no one laughs.

The iron-gated entrance lifts up a little, allowing you all to barrel roll underneath, just before the gates come crashing down again, phew! But only phew for now, as you're not quite sure how you're ever going to get out again!

"Mwah, ha, ha!" you hear echoing through the maze of creepy corridors. Is someone finally laughing at your joke? You follow the sound to a haunted chamber, leaving Dustbin busy nosing around. As you walk, you look at the ground and notice lots of random Halloween objects and costumes scattered about, but then you look up and see . . .

"Avril Le . . ."

"Ahhhhhh!" screams Avril, finishing off her name quite nicely. She is tied to a Tentacle Chair.

"Aha! I've been waiting for you, mwah, ha, ha," laughs Dr. Strangeglove evilly. "I see you got my little lipgloss note!"

"It was a set-up?" you ask.

"You are correct, dear Moshi," replies Dr. Strangeglove. "I knew if I took Avril, the Super Moshis would come looking for her, and I could trap them in the Haunted House, forever, ha, ha! And now I have the rest of the Fizzbangs too, so more Super Moshis will come looking."

Just then, Dustbin walks in, singing one of his number one tunes.

"Dustbin Beaver!" gasps Dr. Strangeglove. "WOW!"

It seems to you like Strangeglove is secretly Beaver's number one fan!

Whilst Strangeglove is momentarily distracted by Dustbin's singing, the Super Moshis zoom over to Avril and untie her. But Strangeglove turns around to see them, just as they are undoing the last knot and quicker than a flash he is there, gripping onto that final knot . . .

"Uh-oh!" you say, realizing you are the only one who can help. "I'd better think quickly."

Just then, you spot two EXTREMELY large and

sticky Spooky Cobwebs in the corner above Strangeglove and an evil Witch Broomstick by your feet. You grab the broom and sweep one of the Spooky Cobwebs down onto Strangeglove's hand.

"Arghhh! That tickles!" shouts the very ticklish Strangeglove, loosening his grip on the knot. The Super Moshis take their chance and untie Avril! Then you, the Super Moshis and Avril race back through the creepy corridors to the iron gate, leaving Dustbin behind.

But the gate is shut solid, so how are you going to get out?

"Your belt!" shouts Thwack.

That's it! You use the buckle on your Super Moshi belt to pick the lock of the gate and get outside to safety.

"Hold on a minute, Dustbin's still in there!" you cry. "You run on ahead and I'll go back in and get him."

Bravely you run back inside the Haunted House to rescue Dustbin. Dr. Strangeglove still has one hand stuck in the web, so you grab Dustbin by the paw and lead him back through the creepy corridors.

Dr. Strangeglove isn't deterred for long and is soon hot on your furry tails, so you run like a scary howling wind. You lay a trap with the second sticky cobweb for Strangeglove to get well and truly stuck into, and race out into the Monstro City streets . . .

Turn to page 19.

The Captain turns around with a start, and suggests you head to the Scare Guitar auditions.

"Of course!" you gasp. "The auditions must've started already, and here I am dilly-dallying around. I need to get there, and fast!"

As you and the Captain race along, you are busy looking at the pavement covered in famous names engraved in the stone, when you see something out of the corner of your eye. It's the luminous smoke signal from before, and it's getting bigger. You stop and stare at it, but then start walking the road to monstar-dom once again, practising your Scare Guitar moves as you go.

You reach the place for the audition and everything is eerily silent.

"What's going on?" you ask. There's no sign of anyone around, not even Simon Growl. "I hope they haven't changed the venue."

"I don't think so," replies the captain.

You're not quite sure why the captain would know anything about the Scare Guitar auditions anyway. Maybe she wants to audition too?

You walk around and around, but there is no one on the music scene.

"Hmm," you say, trying to look intelligent and thoughtful. "I wonder where everyone is. It can't have taken the *CloudyCloth* this long to get here."

"I don't think anything is going to happen tonight,"

says the captain. "How about we go hang out in the Hard Sock Café?"

You stop and think for a minute . . . There will probably be lots of famous celebs hanging out at the Hard Sock Café, maybe you'll even find Avril Le Scream – how cool! On the other foot, the smoke signal is still bothering you, should you go and see if anyone needs your help?

"You coming?" the captain asks you, and once again you are left with a decision.

If you decide to head to the Hard Sock Café and hang out with rockstars, **turn to page 53.**

If you decide you should both jump back on the Gift Island Ferry and head towards the smoke signal, **turn to page 71.** You never know who might need your help.

Super Moshis are GO!

You and the Fizzbangs sign up and change into your bright red masks and capes.

"Super Moshi POWER!" gasps Thwack, waving his drumsticks in the air.

Super Moshied up and raring to go, you, the Fizzbangs and the Super Moshis grab Dustbin Beaver, who is still singing to the Gatekeeper outside, and head back to the Underground Disco to investigate.

First stop, Avril's dressing room.

You pick up a piece of paper with some sort of scrawl written on it in Glueberry Lipgloss. You try to read it, but lots of letters have been scratched off and x's left in their place,

```
Xear Readex,
The Fizzbangx - Monsxxocity
Bxnaxa Montana - The Fall
The xroanas Brothxrs - xrowxiwood
Taylor Miffed - Bred to Toast
The Gxo Fighters - Forget to Walk
Dustbin Beaxer - Viva Ixs Moshis
Lady Gooxxo - Peppy-razzi
Pussycax Poppets - Pipe Down
Broccoli Spears - Pepperxizxr
Xairosniff - Poppxt (Looks xike a Furi)
49 Xence - Catch a Pitch or Try Cryin'
Xxxxx Xx Scream!
```

"It looks like the lipgloss was running out, as it's a bit patchy in places," you explain.

"It could be a message from Avril," says one of the Super Moshis.

"It's just a list of Avril's favourite songs," says DJ Demonsta, "that's not going to help us find her."

"But it appears there are some letters that have been deliberately smudged away," adds another Super Moshi.

"Look!" gasps Riff, interrupting "Sparkly paw prints on the floor! Shall we follow them?"

What should you and the team do next?

If you think the piece of paper has a code to crack on it, **turn to page 23.**

If you decide that the note is just a list of songs and to follow the sparkly paw prints instead, **turn to page 27.**

Picking up the luminous pink lantern, the chamber you are in is transformed into a 1980s school disco, like something your Moshi Ma and Pa might've been to!

You and the Fizzbangs find yourselves transported in time, wearing pink pegwarmers and dancing to Madowner and Bananadramas.

"Why did you pick the pink lantern?" asks Missi Tinkles. "Avril's favourite colour is blue, I'm sure she would've picked that one."

"Oh," you reply, wondering why Missi hadn't thought to mention that fact earlier, "I assumed because of her lipgloss, she must like pink the most." You look around to find a way out, but you are trapped. This time there is no light at the end of the tunnel, just lots of blinking lights and a shiny disco ball on the ceiling.

You are stuck in the eighties and there is nothing you can do. Being a closet eighties music fan, you don't mind all that much. You've always wanted a pair of pink pegwarmers, but the Market Place just never stocked them in your size.

'Well, maybe Avril will come underground looking for eighties inspiration one day, like all the other singers out there,' you think to yourself, 'and we'll be here waiting for her, ready to teach her how to walk like a Moshi!'

THE END

You convince the captain that someone must be in a lot of trouble for there to be such a big smoke signal. You go back to the swanky dock to get back on the Gift Island Ferry. Making time for one quick last visit to the souvenir shop on your way out, you buy a lifetime visitor's pass to the reef.

"This is bound to come in handy next time I visit," you say.

You spot the ferry, and jump onboard, zooming as quickly as you can, towards the signal.

As you get closer, you realize that it's the *Cloudy Cloth Clipper* sinking under the weight of the wannabe Scare Guitarists! None of them ever made it to Rockstar Reef!

"Look!" you cry out, pointing at Simon Growl frantically trying to swim without getting his hair wet.

You dive into Potion Ocean and save as many monsters as you can, whilst the captain gets everyone else onto the lifeboats.

Soon, there is just one monster left in the water. You have your hands full, so you ask the captain to jump in and save the last monster.

"I can't," replies the captain. But the captain has no choice, so jumps in. On reaching the water the captain's sailor outfit comes off to reveal . . .

"It's Avril Le Scream!" cries one of the Scare Guitarists from a lifeboat. The captain was, in fact, Avril in disguise.

Cries of "Wow!" and "Fizzbangtastic!" are heard from the crowds and despite the sinking ship, everyone is happy once again.

Everyone that is, except for poor old Cap'n Buck, who now has a lot of repair work to do, before his next expedition.

"Arrr!" cries out Buck. **"Arrrr, arrrr**, and double **Arrrr!"**

The next day, not only are you branded a hero, for saving the entire clan of Scare Guitarists, Simon Growl and Captain Buck and crew, but you are also given a standing ovation as you walk the streets of Monstro City for bringing Avril back!

All of the auditioners help Cap'n Buck mend the *CloudyCloth.*

At the next Fizzbangs gig, Avril (having finally had a long, well-deserved break in Rockstar Reef) invites you on stage to play Scare Guitar along to all their songs!

'What a rock star I am!' you think very proudly, and you are already planning your next trip to Rockstar Reef.

THE END

Battling through the foam, you and the Fizzbangs (you manage to drag DJ Demonsta away from his decks) find the Emergency Exit sign and barge your way through it.

"Weeeeee!" you cry, finding yourself on an enormous backwards slide, which seems to be taking you upwards out of the underground tunnels.

At the end of the slide you find yourself above ground right by a drain, just off Ooh La Lane.

A little dazed and confused, you look around and see some commotion at the Ice-Scream Shop, but think nothing of it.

You and the Fizzbangs are exhausted from your Underground Tunnels adventure, and need some sleep, so that's what you do.

ZZZZZ!

The next morning, you wake up ready to start searching for Avril again.

'Maybe this time, I'll ask the Super Moshis for help,' you think to yourself.

You grab yourself a delicious breakfast of Jelly Baked Beans and slurp on your Mr. Tea, whilst reading *The Daily Growl*.

The headlines say that Avril was found by the Super Moshis last night and was reunited with her fellow Fizzbangs this morning. (Axl Van Slap had come back with his cat's tail between his legs, realizing one man and his guitar was not the best way to perform and begging to play with the Fizzbangs again.)

You're a little sad you weren't the one to find Avril, but you did get to hang out with your favourite band in the whole of Monstro City. Besides, now there will be music above ground again AND you have no plans for the day, so you can get busy practising for next year's Scare Guitar auditions . . . which you are totally gonna rock!

THE END

You hope that turning right was the 'right' way to go, and that the terrifying creatures had been telling the truth about seeing Avril. Then you hear something,

"Zzz, snort, snort!"

It's Snooze Cruise, snoring away in the tunnel and you know that his snoring will definitely keep the bats away, which is a relief, at least for now.

You and the Fizzbangs march along, and are soon confronted with a Rat Tail Spaghetti junction of tunnels! This time it's more than just right or left you have to choose between!

"What a monster-mix-medley mash-up of tunnels!" cries Demonsta, like only a DJ can. "Where should we go?"

"We need to look for clues," suggests Riff Sawfinger.

"Let's split up," suggests Missi Tinkles.

"Boo, hoo, hoo," cries Thwack, instantly thinking that this is it for his career, it's so hard to get drumming work these days.

"Not split up the band, permanently, Thwack," explains Missi, "Just for now, so we can look for clues."

"Ahhh," sighs Thwack, relieved, but still a little confused, as usual.

Just then, Dustbin Beaver cries out, "Look!"

You look over towards Dustbin and see that he is looking at a pop art wall painting from Monstro City's amateur graffiti artist, Art Lee, (the city's next Dansky wannabe.)

The painting shows a picture of what looks like Avril

holding lots of Bobbing Balloons with the words, 'Lost my voice!' written on them.

"Avril must have lost her voice, and come down here looking for it," you say.

Just then, you see a flash of red – it's the Super Moshis! They must be looking for Avril down here too.

"Let's team up with the Super Moshis," you suggest to everyone.

"But we know Avril and her voice so well," adds DJ Demonsta mixing it up again. "We're more likely to find her."

So, what do you want to do?

If you decide to go with the Super Moshis, **turn to page 38.**

If you decide that the Fizzbangs know Avril better, so will know where to find her and her voice, **turn to page 30.**

"I'm afraid, dear Moshi," says the Elder Furi appearing in a bubble, "All Super Moshi missions are top secret. We could not show you any more of what happened."

"How rubbish!" you reply, disappointed. Just then, Dustbin Beaver comes running in from his private concert for the Gatekeeper outside. (Yes, he had indeed been singing for hours and hours.)

"You called?" Dustbin cries.

"I said rubbish, not Dustbin," you explain, but you decide to tell him the good news that the Super Moshis and the Fizzbangs have found Avril.

"How?" he asks.

"Well, I don't actually know," you reply.

Suddenly a note appears on all the Super Moshi HQ screens,

'Calling all rock fans and wannabe Scare Guitarists! Head back to the Underground Disco right away – the Fizzbangs are back with a bang!'

So you and Dustbin head back underground.

'Well at least Avril is safe and sound,' you think. But really you're a little disappointed. You don't want to miss out on any action again, so you vow to sign up as a Super Moshi as soon as the Fizzbang concert, (oh and the Scare Guitar audition that you are totally gonna win) is over.

THE END

ISBN: 978-1409390541

ISBN: 978-1409390435

ISBN: 978-1409390527

BUSTER'S LOST MOSHLINGS: A Search-and-Find Book

Includes **Secret Code** for an **Ultra Rare Moshling!**

MONSTAR ROOMS HANDBOOK

GAME ON! Tips, Tricks and Cheats for over 40 Moshi Mini Games

Includes **exclusive virtual gift** for your rodant